Brian & Vanita!
Daddy went to
Church this Morning.
There were lots
of people there
but I didn't Draw them

Brian & Vanita!
Daddy operated a big Crane today, I
Loaded Sand in a truck. I wish
I could have put the sand in
your Sand box.

...w a picture
... so good, I'll
... maybe it will
... it you? maybe
... how this one

... will be almost
... this little girl

Vanita's Dedication

This book is dedicated to the memories of:
My father Wilfred Bauknight
My mother Virginia Kelley Bauknight
And also to:
My brother Brian
My sister Clarice

Mike's Dedication

To the brave American families of the United States Military

Acknowledgements

Many thanks to:
Mike Blanc
Kristin Blackwood
David Rozelle
Kurt Landefeld
Paul Royer
Sheila Tarr
Jennie Levy Smith
Michael Olin-Hitt
Elaine Mesek

Postcards from a War
VanitaBooks, LLC
All rights reserved.
© 2009 VanitaBooks, LLC
No part of this book may be reproduced, stored in retrieval systems, or transmitted in any form or through
methods including electronic photocopying, online download, or any other system now known or hereafter
invented – except by reviewers, who may quote brief passages in a review to be printed in a newspaper
or print or online publication – without express written permission from VanitaBooks, LLC.
Text by Vanita Oelschlager.
Illustrations by Mike Blanc and Wilfred Bauknight.
Design by Mike Blanc.

Printed in China.
Hardcover Edition ISBN 978-0-9800162-9-1
Paperback Edition ISBN 978-0-9819714-0-7

www.VanitaBooks.com

U.S. ARMY POSTAL SERVICE

OCT
08
1945

A.P.O.

Postcards
from a War

Vanita Oelschlager

Illustrations by Mike Blanc and
Colonel Wilfred Bauknight U.S.A.R.

My name is Matthew Brian Jackson. My dad has a job downtown. My mom has a job in the Air Force. Mom had to go to another country because there's a war going on. After school, I go to my Grandpa's house and wait for Dad to pick me up. Grandpa's name is Brian, like my middle name.

I love my grandpa. We talk about a lot of things. I told him I was sad because Mom had gone away to this war. Then he told me a story that made me feel a little better.

"Matthew, when I was six years old, my dad had to go away to war. It was more than 60 years ago, and it was called World War II. Have you learned about that in school yet?"

I said, "Yes."

"When he said he had to go away, I wasn't sure what that meant. And neither did my younger sisters Vanita and Clarice. But my mom, your great-grandmother, did. She knew that when men went away to war sometimes they didn't come back."

"I remember when he had to leave we took him to the train station. In those days soldiers traveled from their homes to military bases by train. Then all the soldiers took trains together from their bases to seaports where big ships took them to the war.

"Some soldiers went east to New York and got on ships that took them to Europe. Dad's train took him to San Francisco in California. He boarded a ship that took him from California all the way to the Philippine Islands."

Grandpa put his arm around me and then said, "Before he left, Dad looked at me and said I was now the man of the house and I had to be the brave one. No crying. And I had to help take care of my little sisters. He said he would come back home. But he didn't know when.

"I didn't cry when he got on the train. Neither did my mom. But when the train left, she started to cry. My sisters cried because my mom was crying. I cried too, just a little."

I told my grandpa, "I didn't cry when Mom left. But, sometimes I cry now. I cry when I think of what can happen to my mother so far away from home. I cry when I think that she might not come home."

"Yes, Matthew, I understand that. Sometimes I cried too. But never in front of Mom or my sisters. When I was young, people thought you needed to hide your feelings. Now, we all know it is better to let your feelings out."

"Were you scared, Grandpa?"

"One time I went to the movies with a friend. In those days, no one had TVs and the only way you could get news about the war was from newspapers and radios and something called 'newsreels.' Newsreels were like movies that showed before the regular movie started.

"The one I saw showed planes dropping bombs and cities on fire and people running away. It was very scary because now I knew that my dad could be going someplace where bombs might get dropped on him."

"Did your dad come home?"

"Yes, Matthew. He came home after the war was over. But he also did something that made it a lot easier to wait for him. I want to show you something. Follow me."

Grandpa got up and started going upstairs. I followed him. Then he went up the stairs to the attic. It was dark up there and a little scary. It smelled funny, like dirty clothes all piled up. Grandpa turned on a light and walked over to an old trunk. He opened it and looked for a second, then pulled out a stack of old letters. Then he closed the trunk and sat down on it.

"Come, Matthew, I want to show you something I haven't looked at in a long time."

Grandpa untied the string and looked at the envelope on top.

The Bauknight Family –
Virginia, Brian, Vanita and Clarice
312 Newburn Drive
Pittsburgh 16, Pa. USA

"My dad started sending us letters while he was away. He knew as long as he sent letters that we would know he was alright.

"This is the first letter he sent. See the postmark? San Francisco, California. We got this about a week after he left us."

Grandpa pulled the letter out and read it. But he didn't say anything. Then he pulled out the next one. It looked different. It was a postcard with a picture of a ship that Great Grandpa had drawn. He read this one.

BRIAN & VANITA:
DADDY WENT DOWN BY THE PIER TODAY AND SAW A BIG SHIP LOADED WITH MEN GOING HOME. DADDY WANTED TO GO TOO, BUT WILL HAVE TO WAIT AWHILE. I LOVE YOU.
LOVE
DADDY

Look at it from this direction →

"Brian and Vanita, Daddy went down by the pier today and saw a big ship loaded with men going home. Daddy wanted to go too, but will have to wait awhile. I love you. Love Daddy"

Grandpa handed me some other postcards.

"Why did he call you Johnny Pig?" I asked.

"Oh, that was his way of playing with us. He liked to pull on our toes and say, 'This little piggy went to market. This little piggy stayed home. This little piggy ate roast beef. This little piggy had none. And this little piggy cried, "wee, wee, wee" all the way home.'

"I was Johnny Pig. Vanita was Freddy Pig and Clarice was Willie Pig."

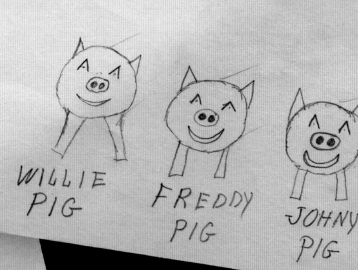

"OK. Here's one in an envelope. Feel how thin the paper is? That's because sending all that mail back to the United States weighed a lot and cost a lot. So, he wrote on thin paper that didn't cost much to mail. So did everybody else.

I BET BRIAN + VANITA SCARED MAMA + CLARICE ON HALLOWEEN!

"On October 20, 1944 he wrote: 'I bet Brian &

Another letter said: "I know it's cool at home because it's fall. It's fall here too. But it feels like summer. That's because the Philippines are close to the equator. Has Mama showed you where the islands are on our globe? I am helping people rebuild a bridge. I drew pictures showing how big it should be. The people here work very hard. They want to make their city beautiful again."

A postcard said: "Daddy ran one of these big tractors today. It is called a bulldozer. Love, Daddy."

Grandpa read more of the postcards and letters to me. He flipped through them slowly and finally got to the last one.

"This one is my favorite, Matthew. 'I jumped with delight when they said: Major Bauknight, you are going home.'"

"Did my Mom ever see these letters and postcards, Grandpa?"

U.S.A.R.

MAJOR BAUKNIGHT

"Yes she did, Matthew. We talked about them when she was young. After that I forgot about them until today. She especially liked the ones where my dad would tell of all the wonderful things we would do together when he got home."

He looked through the pack again and pulled out her favorite. "Brian, Vanita, and Clarice: When I get home I will build you a tent in your play yard. I will make it out of my mosquito net."

BRIAN, VANITA, AND CLARICE: When I get home I will Build you a Tent in your play yard. I will Make it out of My Mosquito Net.

"I don't like war, Grandpa. Why is there war? Why did Mom want to go to fight in the war?"

"I don't like war either, Matthew. I have always wished there were a peaceful way to settle world problems."

"But why did my mother have to go? She never told me."

"She believes in protecting this country and what it stands for. It's more than a job for her, Matthew.

"She believes that your world will be better if we can stop people and nations from hurting each other.

"My dad believed that too. He was fighting for his country.

"He thought his country was right, and we needed to fight for what was right."

"But, isn't war people hurting other people?"
I asked.

"You're right, Matthew. War is always about people hurting other people. Sometimes wars are fought because people have been taught to hate others not like themselves; some wars are fought to steal other peoples' land or freedom.

"We adults admit that we do not have all the answers. Sometimes it doesn't make sense. I hope that you and your friends can find the answers that we could not find."

"Grandpa, do you think Mom will remember
how important those postcards and letters were?
Do you think she'll mail me from the war?"

"Well, Matthew, I think she just might. Maybe you should start checking your mailbox."

"But Grandpa, there are cell phones now so maybe she'll call me. They have tents where she can talk to me, and I can see her. She can also send me notes and pictures on her computer. What if she sends me letters and pictures on the computer mailbox? Wouldn't that be great?"

"However she sends them, Matthew, we can make a book together. We'll use my cards and letters from World War II, and you can use your e-mail from your mom's war. We will make a book together. It will be our "Love, Daddy" and "Love, Mom" book. Would you like that?"

It wasn't long until I got my first picture letter from Mom on my computer.

Just like Brian had been Johnny Pig, and Vanita had been Freddy Pig and Clarice Willie Pig, Mom sent me a drawing where I was Matthew Pig. She *had* remembered the letters and cards that had been so important to Grandpa and his sisters.

MATTHEW PIG

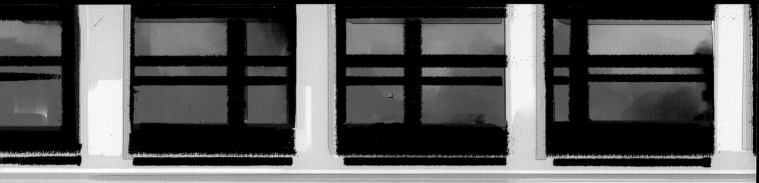

Grandpa and I made that book with the old pictures and the new ones.

I told Grandpa, that I loved our book, but that when I grew up, I hoped there wouldn't ever be wars anymore. I asked Grandpa if he thought that was possible.

"Matthew," he said, "if anyone can make that happen, it will be you and your friends. And you can always count on me to help you."

Vanita Oelschlager is a wife, mother, grandmother, philanthropist, former teacher, current caregiver, author and poet. She is a graduate of Mt. Union College in Alliance, Ohio, where she currently serves as a Trustee. Vanita is also Writer in Residence for the Literacy Program at The University of Akron. She and her husband Jim received a Lifetime Achievement Award for the National Multiple Sclerosis Society in 2006. She won the Congressional 'Angels in Adoption' Award for the state of Ohio in 2007 and was named National Volunteer of the Year by the MS Society in 2008.

Like Natalie Cole sang a song with her father, Nat King Cole, years after his death, Vanita has written this book with her father's help 30 years after his death.

Wilfred Bauknight was born in western South Carolina in 1910 and graduated with a degree in Civil Engineering from the University of South Carolina in 1932. He met his wife Virginia on a blind date. They moved to Pittsburgh in 1935. Wilfred became deeply involved with the Army Corps of Engineers, his local church and –especially– his family over the next twenty years.

The army would not accept his civilian status during the war, so he became a part of the active Reserves in the early 1940s. He was assigned to active duty in the Philippines in mid-1945. The war with Japan ended as he was on his way by ship in August 1945. He remained on duty and sent home many letters and self-made postcards during the six months he was stationed in Manila.

These letters capture not only a father's desire to ease the fears felt by his wife and three children during his absence, but also the early post-war efforts to begin the reconstruction of a city devastated by nearly four years of war.

When Wilfred returned home in early 1946, he resumed his responsibilities as husband and father. In addition he continued to serve in the Army Corps of Engineers, retiring with the rank of Colonel.

Wilfred Bauknight died in March of 1979.

Mike Blanc is a life-long professional artist. His work has illuminated countless publications for both corporate and public interests, worldwide. Accomplished in traditional drawing and painting techniques, he now works almost exclusively in digital medium. His first book, *Francesca*, was written by Vanita Oelschlager and published in Autumn, 2008. *Postcards from a War* is their second collaboration.

About the art: Wilfred Bauknight sent home many letters and postcards that included his illustrations while on active duty in the Philippines in 1945-6. Wilfred was an engineer, skilled in draftsmanship. The illustrations he included with his correspondence look like they were "engineered" - a lot of detail!

Mike Blanc's illustrations for the story compliment Wilfred's postcards with paintings in two categories: sepia toned to represent the recollections of Grandfather's past, and full color to depict the present. The paintings were produced with Corel® Painter™ digital painting software for artists.

Profits: Fisher House Foundation, Inc. is a not-for-profit organization dedicated to helping America's military families in their time of need. The Foundation builds "comfort homes" at the campuses of major military and VA hospitals, enabling families to be close to a sick or injured loved one. Fisher Houses are beautifully decorated homes with 7 to 21 suites, a common kitchen, laundry facilities, spacious dining room, and an inviting living room, with library and toys for children.

Through the generous support of the American public, the Foundation covers all costs to stay at an Army, Air Force or Navy Fisher House (there has never been a charge to stay at a VA Fisher House). No one pays to stay at a Fisher House. We truly believe that a family's love is the best medicine!

Fisher House Foundation provides a "home away from home" that enables America's military families to be close to a loved one during sickness or injury.

All net profits from this book will benefit Fisher House Foundation

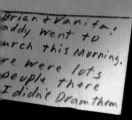

Brian & Vanita:
addy went to
urch this Murning.
re were luts
peuple there
I didn't Dram them

a big Crane today, I
ck. I wish